I0668872

l i r uy ami up dr Ahdp v

Making a Rock Garden

l i r uy ami up dr Ahdp v

Making a Rock Garden

JaBS 3FAS © 688886994696

Uun xi h n Fyus t i / b aA/ Cdr dhd/ Ay vxudood/ Ndt dr

Cs : i u@sxs 5 Ar hui dv l ndbi ek 3 t n i os 1hi

P su i d: dnedbó bs s k v dx **www.hansebooks.com**

MAKING A
ROCK GARDEN

THE
HOUSE & GARDEN
<u>*MAKING*</u>
BOOKS

It is the intention of the publishers to make this series of little volumes, of which *Making a Rock Garden* is one, a complete library of authoritative and well illustrated handbooks dealing with the activities of the home-maker and amateur gardener. Text, pictures and diagrams will, in each respective book, aim to make perfectly clear the possibility of having, and the means of having, some of the more important features of a modern country or suburban home. Among the titles already issued or planned for early publication are the following: *Making a Rose Garden; Making a Lawn; Making a Tennis Court; Making a Fireplace; Making Paths and Driveways; Making a Poultry House; Making a Garden with Hotbed and Coldframe; Making Built-in Bookcases, Shelves and Seats; Making a Garden to Bloom This Year; Making a Water Garden; Making a Garden of Perennials; Making the Grounds Attractive with Shrubbery; Making a Naturalized Bulb Garden;* with others to be announced later.

A nearly buried boulder is easily converted into a beautiful little rock garden. Fill in depressions with soil and plant there and around the edges of the boulder *Phlox subulata*, sedum, arabis, etc.

MAKING A ROCK GARDEN

By H. S. ADAMS

NEW YORK

McBRIDE, NAST & COMPANY

1912

Copyright, 1912, by
McBRIDE, NAST & CO.

Published May, 1912

CONTENTS

PAGE

THE ILLUSTRATIONS

FACING

PAGE

Making a Rock Garden

THE ROCK GARDEN

In Europe, particularly in England, the rock garden is an established institution with a distinct following. The English works on the subject alone form a considerable bibliography.

On this side of the Atlantic, the rock garden is so little understood that it is an almost unconsidered factor in the beautifying of the home grounds. There are a few notable rock gardens in this country, all on large estates, and in more instances some excellent work has been done on a smaller and less complicated scale either by actual creation or by taking advantage of natural opportunities. But for the most part America has confined its rock garden vision principally to the so-called "rockery."

Now a rockery, with all the good intentions lying behind it, is not a rock garden. It is no more a rock garden than a line of cedars planted in an exact circle would be a wood. A rockery is generally a lot of stones stuck in a pile of soil or, worse yet, a circular array of stones filled in with soil.

A rock garden, above all else, is not artificial; at least, so far as appearance goes. It is a garden with rocks. The rocks may be few or many, they may have been disposed by nature or the hand of man; but always the effect is naturalistic, if not actually natural. The rock garden's one and only creed is nature.

Rock gardens are of so many legitimate—in other words, natural—types, that there is not the slightest excuse for a rockery. Even that commonest of excuses, finding a use for stray stones, falls to the ground. Any close observer of nature is familiar with these types. The natural rock gardens range from the patches of alpine plants above the timber line in high mountains down the lower slopes and through defiles to fields on or near sea level. Not infrequently they come down to the very sea, while sweet waters commonly define and, what is better, are now and then incorporated in, them—here a pool, there a brook. The bog, too, the heath and the desert, they take unto themselves, though perhaps only the nearer edge. And does man, by ponderous effort, raise up massive masonry in orderly fashion; one day disorder comes and nature makes things look natural by another kind of rock garden. Rome's Coliseum and the ruins of Kenilworth Castle are only two of the unnumbered examples of this.

Here, in a nutshell, are not only the natural variations of the rock garden, but the inspiration. No rock garden worthy of the name has ever been created by man that did not depend upon a study of those that nature has given the world in prodigal abundance. There were the why and the how of it all, and man simply saw and made use of his observations.

The advantages of a rock garden are, primarily, an element of picturesqueness that nothing else can provide, and the possession of a place in which can be grown some of the loveliest flowers on earth that, if they flourish at all, will never do as well in the ordinary garden as in conditions more or less approximating their natural habitat. Also it may be made a pleasance of extraordinary attractiveness. Occasionally—and here is one of the most important things to be learned about the rock garden—it is the veritable key to the garden situation; there are small places where no other kind is worth while, if indeed it is possible.

THE CHOICE OF A SITE

The best site for a rock garden is where it ought to be. That is a sad truth, for it eliminates some homes from the game; but useless waste of time will be saved if this is recognized at the outset. First cast your eye about and see if you have a spot where a rock garden would look as if it belonged there; that is the supreme test. If one does not seem to belong there, give up the idea philosophically and take it out in enjoying the rock gardens of other people.

As a rule a rock garden should not be near the house; it is something savoring of the wild that does not fit in with most architecture. Exceptions are when the house is on a rocky site that makes such planting desirable, if not imperative, and a slope from the rear or one side of a house that seems decided enough to permit of a sharp break in the general landscape treatment. Save in these circumstances, it is better that it should not be in sight of the house. This is not so hard as it sounds; even on a small place, the spot is easily concealed by a planting of shrubbery.

Nor should the rock garden, any more than the rockery, be in the lawn unless it is depressed and therefore out of sight, or mainly so, from the level. The depression may be a natural or an artificial one, it may be a brook with high banks or it may be a sunken pathway. The edge of a lawn is better, a corner of it is better yet, and preferable to either is a bank sloping down from it. The bank on either side of steps leading from one lawn level to another is also a possibility to be considered.

Trees need not be altogether avoided; sometimes they are essential to the pictorial effect. It is not well, however, to place a rock garden near very large trees. The drip is bad, especially for alpines, and the greedy roots not only rob the plants of nourishment but are very apt to dislocate the stones.

Wherever possible make the entrance to the rock garden a
rough flight of steps. Excavate if necessary. Plant the step
crevices as well as those of the side walls

Somewhere just outside the real garden is the best place; then it is only a step from one little world into another that is altogether different. If the rock garden leads to a bit of wood, either directly or through a wild garden, there will be all the more to rejoice over. The more irregularity the site has, or suggests, the better; a rock garden not only should have no straight lines, but it is not well that all of it should be comprehended in a single view—no matter whether the area be large or small.

What constitutes a good site is well illustrated by one of the existing American rock gardens. The place is large, and in the rear of the house the grounds are level for a considerable distance and then drop with a fairly steep bank to a driveway, below which another terrace leads to a meadow. Instead of being continuous, however, the bank above the driveway is broken by a little glen, seemingly leading nowhere, but actually an entrance to both the rear lawn and the formal garden. In this glen is the rock garden, or rather the main part of it. Though bounded on the north— it runs east and west—by the formal garden and on the south by the lawn, the rock garden can be seen from neither of these, nor from the house. It is conveniently near all three, yet distinctly apart from all. A thin planting of evergreens screens it on the south and east sides, and there is a low hedge between it and the formal garden. The rock garden overflows the glen and runs along the bank on either side, the shady section being devoted to an extensive collection of hardy ferns. Across the driveway there is more rock garden and then a short stretch of dry wall garden. Such a site as this does not have to be found all made. Given any grounds with a bank, and a little imagination, and a glen is a mere matter of shoveling soil. Call it a gorge, if you prefer. Either, in miniature, is a favored rock garden form; so are hill and crest.

Thus far the assumption has been that the rocks have to be gathered up from various parts of the place or brought in from the outside. But many grounds, especially those of country places, have the rocks; often more than are wanted. Although sometimes this is the best of luck, now and then the trouble of blasting and rearranging is about as great as if all the stone had to be found. It does, nevertheless, make easier the choice of a site; where rocks are naturally, there they ought to be. Occasionally the rocks are so disposed that there is no choice; the site settles itself and it is up to you to make the most of it.

A single boulder, a few scattered rocks, or a rocky bank can be converted into a simple rock garden without moving a stone. A little judicious planting and the transformation is complete.

A rock garden with water is a rock garden glorified. Wherever possible, without injury to the main scheme, the garden should be brought to the water. Failing that, bring the water to it, if this is practicable; which can be determined when the site is picked out.

THE WORK OF CONSTRUCTION

Spring is the best time to make a rock garden. When the important matter of the proper site has been put in the past, a definite scheme must be planned. Upon the definiteness of this scheme, much of the success of the rock garden will depend. Here desire will have to be subservient to the situation. It is not so much what you want as what is best in the circumstances.

Do not attempt slavishly to copy the rock garden of some one else. All the money in the world would not create an exact duplicate for you, since nature has made no two rocks precisely alike. Study them, of course; get all the ideas you can. But study first, and most, nature—more particularly its ways in your own neighborhood. Anywhere there is abundant opportunity. Take a leaf or two from the book of the Japanese gardeners. They are past-masters of the art of making rock gardens, with a bit of water thrown in. They make use of comparatively few blossoming plants, but their example is invaluable in the disposition of rocks with simple effectiveness, in the simulation of height and distance, in the proper employment of turf, and in the planting of such small trees and shrubs as are suitable for a rock garden scheme.

Measure carefully the space at command, and then lay out the plan on cross-ruled paper. Call each of the little squares a square foot and the labor will be made easy. Next, figure out a good entrance, and, if possible, an equally good exit— the one invisible from the other. Then outline the main path, which should be as devious as the situation allows, and, if byways cannot be added, provide for bays, or more pronounced recesses. Remember that you are not merely to simulate nature; you are, by a process of compressing much in little, to epitomize it.

Then comes the selection of the rocks. Usually the rock close at hand, perhaps on the very grounds, will answer every purpose. If you are not fortunate enough to own any, very likely there is more than one townsman who will be glad to give you all the boulders and smaller rocks that you want, if you will only remove them from spots where they are not desired. The cost of removal, even in the case of boulders of fair size, is not great.

Barring quartz rock, which does not look well, almost any kind of natural stone may be made use of to the best advantage. Artificial stone should be shunned like the plague. Limestone and sandstone are good materials; granite is better. Granite, however, does not stratify, and if stratified effects are desired, another stone must be selected. A good plan is to use more than one kind, but to keep them properly apart. Weather-beaten granite is excellent material, and, in general, it is well to have the rock look anything but newly quarried. Pick out some rocks with a growth of lichen on them, and be sure that this is not disturbed by the moving.

Good rock garden planting. Each of the principal species has a soil pocket to itself. Note the effective background and irregular crevices

Boulders may run up to several tons in weight. Where none is readily obtainable, one can be simulated by ingeniously combining a few small ones and concealing the joints by the planting of such things as stonecrops in earth—which, save in rare cases of sheer necessity, is always used in the construction of a rock garden in place of mortar.

If the site is level, the next step is to change all that—first on paper. Unless the lay of the land is all right at the outset, the configuration of the rock garden must not depend wholly upon the upbuilding; there must be some excavations, but no depressions deep enough to catch and hold water just where you will want to walk.

Aside from the path levels, building begins with the rocks, not with the soil. This is a highly important point. Place the boulders first; they are the big effects. Aside from that, the heaviest work will be out of the way. Then start in with the outlining base rocks. These should be placed with the

16

largest surface to the ground and should vary in size. It is not essential that the lowest rocks should be slightly buried in the ground, but that course is preferable.

When the paths and outer margins have been thus defined, scatter more rocks over the intervening surface, placing them fairly thick but not close together. Next, fill in with soil, packing it firmly and ramming it hard into every crevice. If it fits in with the day's work, it is not a bad plan to water the rock work well in order to pack the soil, and when resuming the labor on the morrow, to add more soil, well pressed down, before proceeding with the second layer of rock.

This second layer should have the rocks placed with the front edge slightly back from that of the lower row in order to form a slope, though an occasional overhang may be fashioned if required for a certain plant known to abhor a drip from above. The construction then proceeds as before, until the desired height is reached. The height is entirely arbitrary, but some points should be at least as high as the line of vision, as one of the great advantages of a rock garden is the pleasure of enjoying some of the typical rock plants without stooping. The rocks used as fillers should overlap here and there to give strength, but care must be taken to contrive plenty of long soil runs. Eighteen inches should be the very least. A plant like the alpine androsace is a tiny rosette, seemingly requiring no more than an inch or two of soil, but its roots are likely to be found following an earth-filled crevice in the rocks to the depth of a yard or so. It is because of this deep penetration of roots that the soil should be packed so very firm; the roots must be in no danger of loose soil or of striking a hidden hollow.

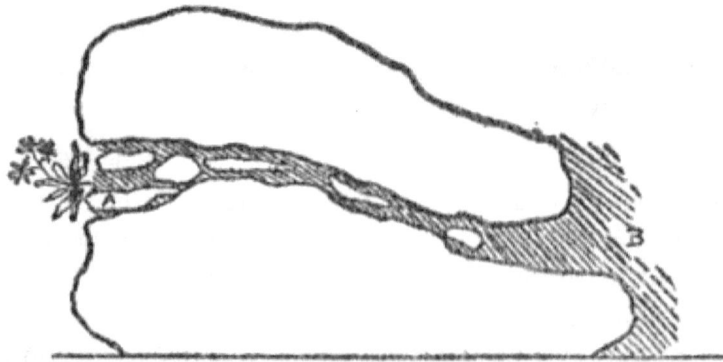

Where a rock would bear too heavily on the one below it, even with soil between, the pressure may be relieved by the use of small stones. The soil run need not be straight, but it must be continuous, so that the roots of the plant may find their way from A through to B

At no point between two stones should the layer of soil be less than two or three inches thick after being packed hard. If an upper stone is likely to bear down too heavily and crush the plant roots, this may be avoided by placing small stones here and there in the layer of soil. The roots will work between these stones, but there must be a continuous, though not necessarily straight, soil run from the front of the rock work to the solid filling of earth. The run should slope downward slightly.

Rocks calculated to simulate a natural stratification ought to be laid on an incline for proper drainage. Such pieces of rock may also be employed sparsely in wedging, and in the making of the so-called "pockets."

These pockets are of prime importance in the construction of a rock garden. They hold the only considerable spaces of soil and are the chief means of colonizing plants, thus providing for pronounced color effects. They should break the slopes and be irregular in size, shape, and distribution. The large ones may be easily subdivided by small stones when the

18

planting is done if a further separation of species is desirable. The soil must slope a little from the top, so that there will be no standing water.

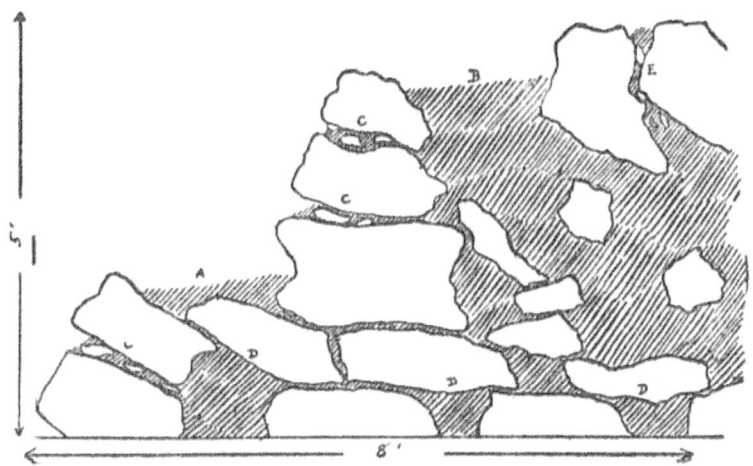

Cross-section of rock garden construction, showing shallow (A) and deep (B) soil pockets; tilting and wedging of rocks (C); bridging (D), and perpendicular crevice soil run (E). Two to three inches of soil between all joints. The lowest rocks are partly buried

The drainage of a rock garden is of vital importance. There must be plenty of moisture stowed away behind the rocks against the heat of summer, but all excess must be carried away. The garden should drain naturally, as the hills do. If any doubt exists, make a drainage bed of eight inches of clinkers before starting to lay the stones.

The soil should be a good loam with a little peat, and stones varying in size from a mustard seed to an almond. A little manure may be used, but it must be old.

PLANTING THE GARDEN

There are two ways of planting a rock garden. One is to do all the crevice planting along with the building, and the other, of course, is to defer everything until the rocks are in place and the soil thoroughly settled.

The former plan is a singularly appealing, as well as practical, one. There is something fascinating in finishing completely a part of the work as one goes along. The practical advantage lies chiefly in the fact that by this method good-sized plants may be firmly established in crevices at the very outset. The soil in that case should be put part way in the crevice and packed down. Then some loose soil sprinkled on top, and the plant, with the earth well shaken from the roots, unless it has a tap root, laid down horizontally with the crown just outside the edge of the soil. Next spread the roots to follow the soil run; fill up the crevice with more soil, packed well, and follow with more plants of the same kind. Use small stones to wedge plants where it appears necessary. Plants that hang down should be placed in the higher crevices; this must be all thought out beforehand.

As a matter of fact, the planting plan cannot be too thoroughly thought out in advance. At point after point it dovetails with the structural plan, which must accord with the requirements of what may be called the more difficult rock plants—the alpines, some of the ferns, and those plants that fit in well with rock work but demand more than the ordinary garden moisture. The best way is to decide what plants are most desirable in the circumstances, omitting, as a rule, the difficult or "finicky" ones; there will be plenty of time to experiment with those when you have more

21

experience. Make a face plan of the several sections of the rock work and mark on it where the plants are to go. Use numbers, each corresponding to a species.

Where only a small effect is desired, a tongue of rock work like this is an easy solution of the problem. Note the avoidance of straight lines

The general idea is that all the soil shall be concealed, not necessarily at the moment of planting, but at the end of one or two seasons' growth. Unless you are a collector, variety is of little importance. The main thing is that there shall be beauty as a whole, a few marked seasonal effects of color with massed bloom and some green the year round; the garden must never be bare at any time, as nature will show you. Plants clustered here and single there is a good planting rule. Colonies, always of marked irregularity, ought to merge into one another, but they should not so overrun the rock work that no stones are in sight. Not infrequently some of the best effects are obtained where more rock than flowers is seen. A boulder, for example, calls for the contrast of plants, perhaps only a few low-growing ones in a natural pocket, rather than a semi-eclipse. As a rule, plant one hundred of half a dozen or so suitable, and easy, species in preference to fifty or more kinds.

22

Study at the same time the form of the plants that are to be used; some quickly resolve themselves into a carpet, some never get beyond mere tufts, some always grow straight up, some prefer to hang down, and some have foliage that is evergreen or nearly so. To be more specific, one plant of *Saponaria ocymoides* will spread out over four square feet of soil, and thus fill completely a moderate-sized pocket, whereas to conceal the same amount of ground three dozen auriculas might have to be used. The same is true of the white rock cress (*Arabis albida*). So, too, with a crevice. A single plant of one of the trailing stonecrops would fill it, perhaps, when a number of rosettes of the smaller kinds of house leek would be called for.

Tall plants, like the foxglove, may sometimes be used, in a small group, at the end of a bay on the level of the path; but they are best placed behind the rock work, as a background, or as dominating features of the entrance or exit of the garden. At the entrance or exit such bold plants make a good bridge between the rock garden and the outer grounds. Spreading and trailing plants should be placed a foot or more above the path level and most plants with tufts or rosettes of foliage. If the path is broad enough some of the wide-spreading plants may go at the base of the rocks, but the rule there is to use those of moderate spread, with a few tufted plants and some that grow upright, but are not tall, to lend variety. When the path is of flat stones, irregular in both size and placing, this growth should fill all the soil space—even between the stones. Such a path will be found more than worth while, and not as much of an undertaking as it may seem.

Obvious considerations are that plants with a decided hankering after moisture or shade should be favored in the matter of location, though it is astonishing how adaptive many of them are.

Do not plant the weak next to the strong. Unless you are a gardener of eternal vigilance, the weak will have the worst of it before you realize what a mistake you have made.

Finally, do not forget that planting is not the end; it is only the beginning—of planting. So long as the rock garden exists there will always be planting. Normal mortality will necessitate some, there will be thinning out, and time will suggest additions and more or less rearrangement.

And with the planting goes on the continual care, much of which can be done in the course of the daily walk in the garden, and therefore the loss of time will not be felt. Water in case of a real drought, but use a sprinkler, and do not stop until the ground has been soaked to a depth of a few inches. Mere surface watering is bad enough in the ordinary garden; in a rock garden it is a fatal error, as the growth of roots near the top of the soil leaves the plants in no condition to stand the full force of the summer sun.

Go over the garden thoroughly once a year and all the time keep a sharp lookout for weeds. If the soil is heavy, top-dress with grit in the fall. Grit is good for rock plants. Stone chips placed around a plant will prevent too much dampness lodging about the collar in winter. Watch out for weak spots after very heavy rains.

PLANTS FOR A ROCK GARDEN

So many plants are suitable for a rock garden that the range of choice is bewildering. In this, as in the laying out of the garden, advisability takes precedence over pure personal desire, though, very fortunately, it is often not difficult to make the two go hand in hand; a little intelligent thought helps a lot.

To the beginner, no better advice can be given than that which applies to the picking out of the rocks—use the material which is close at hand. This is not, by any means, a mere suggestion to follow the lines of least resistance. It is far more. In the first place, there is always an endless amount of beautiful and suitable plant life to be had without going far afield. Then again, natural harmonious effects in your immediate neighborhood are pretty sure to be appropriate to your grounds. Finally, you can see for yourself how things grow, and as for the hardiness of plants, you have it already tested for you. This refers not alone to the natural conditions; there is a second wide field in the gardens—the hardy gardens—of others, where you can at once choose from the many and learn whether certain plants are too tender or require too much care for your use.

So far as plants native to the immediate neighborhood are concerned, their value to the rock garden of the average person with limited time, who is not obsessed with the idea of growing the rare and curious, cannot be overestimated. And they are so many; more than most realize, and often of an individual beauty not always appreciated in the bewildering profusion of the wild but plainly apparent when an individual, or a little group, is open to close study in a rock garden. Do not make the rather common mistake of thinking that they are too familiar to be interesting; they are never likely to be. And, honestly, can you say in your heart that they are?

Native plants are excellent material for the rock garden.

**The foam flower (*Tiarella cordifolia*) at the top, and one of
the smaller ferns at the bottom**

For a Connecticut rock garden the Greek valerian
(*Polemonium reptans*) must be purchased, unless a neighbor
can spare some from his collection of old-fashioned flowers;
there it belongs in that category. But why should you of
Minnesota or Missouri deny so beautiful a flower a place in
your rock garden, simply because you have only to go to
the woods for it? The English enthusiast brings home
primroses from the Himalayas, gentians from the Swiss
Alps, and *Dryas Drummondi* from the Canadian Rockies for
his rock garden, but he does not fail to take advantage of
some of the common things near-by—even the "pale
primrose" and the cowslip.

From ferns alone, or from only plants of shrubby growth, a
most beautiful native rock garden may be made. And adding
small flowering plants, or excluding all else, there are
limitless opportunities. It goes without saying that A's rock
garden in Maine will not be like B's in Louisiana; but there
is no law compelling it to be.

Among the common wild flowers of the East that take on
unexpected new beauty when transferred to the rock garden
are the celandine (*Chelidonium majus*), strawberry (*Fragaria
Virginica*), cranesbill (*Geranium maculatum*), toadflax (*Linaria
vulgaris*), orange hawkweed (*Hieracium auranticum*), herb
Robert (*Geranium Robertianum*), coltsfoot (*Tussilago Farfara*),
Solomon's seal (*Polygonatum biflorum*), foam flower (*Tiarella
cordifolia*), bloodroot (*Sanguinaria Canadensis*), and some of
the violets. These are but a few names, and random ones at
that. Some of them, the coltsfoot, cranesbill, celandine, and
toadflax, spread too rapidly, but by careful watching and
not allowing the seed to ripen, they may be kept within
bounds. There are many such plants that will take all the

room in sight if they are allowed to, and they must be watched closely, or else discarded altogether. Some of them answer a good purpose by giving the rock garden a quick start, after which they may easily be reduced or thrown out altogether. There need be no compunction about discarding. Certain plants, like certain friends, you enjoy having for a visit, but do not care to see remain forever and a day.

Annuals as a class are not desirable for the rock garden; for one thing, the care of renewal is too great. Biennials are almost as much care, but in each case there will always be exceptions that are a matter of individual preference. Few, for example, would have the heart to reject the dainty little purple toadflax of Switzerland (*Linaria alpina*), just because it is a biennial. The main dependence, however, must be placed on perennials—the plants that, barring accidents, last indefinitely. These should be mostly species; if horticultural, do not use the bizarre—Darwin tulips, for example, or the Madame Chereau iris. Nor, with rare exceptions, should double flowers be used. A double daffodil looks horribly out of place, while the double white rock cress (*Arabis albida*) will pass.

The easy rock garden plants, where the material is not taken from the wild, are to be found in most of the large hardy gardens of the East. Some of them are natives of Europe or Asia, and more than is commonly suspected are at home in other parts of the United States. Among the best of these for carpets of bloom are *Phlox subulata*, *Phlox amœna*, *Aubrietia deltoidea*, maiden pink (*Dianthus deltoides*), blue bugle (*Ajuga Genevensis*), white bugle (*Ajuga reptans*), woolly chickweed (*Cerastium tomentosum*), creeping thyme (*Thymus serpyllum*), dwarf speedwell (*Veronica repens*), *Saponaria ocymoides*, alpine mint (*Calamintha alpina*), and pink, white, and yellow stonecrops (sedum). All of them fairly hug the ground.

There are other plants that form a carpet of foliage, but the flower stalks rise higher. These include white rock cress (*Arabis albida*), the permissible double buttercup (*Ranunculus acris fl. pl.*), the also permissible double German catchfly (*Lychnis viscaria*), another double flower, "fair maids of France" (*Ranunculus aconitifolius*), Carpathian bellflower (*Campanula Carpatica*), grass pink (*Dianthus plumarius*), *Iris pumila*, crested iris (*Iris cristata*), Christmas rose (*Helleborus niger*), *Phlox divaricata*, *Phlox ovata*, *Phlox repens*, foam flower (*Tiarella cordifolia*), *Veronica incana*, *Alyssum saxatile*, *Saxifraga cordifolia*, and various avens (geum).

Several of the primulas give a like effect if the planting is close—as it should be in a pocket. The best are the English primrose (*Primula vulgaris*), cowslip (*P. veris*), oxlip (*P. elatior*), bird's eye (*P. farinosa*), yellow auricula (*P. auricula*), *P. denticulata*, and *P. Cortusoides*. Similarly, spring bulbs may be employed; plant them, for the most part, under a ground cover so that the soil will not show when they die down. Of the tulips, single ones of the early and cottage types may be used, if in a solid color, but most to be preferred are the species, such as the sweet yellow (Florentine) tulip of Southern Europe and the little lady tulip (*Tulipa Clusiana*). Crocuses are also best in type forms, and the small, single, yellow trumpet kinds are the finest daffodil material. Single white or blue hyacinths may be used, but better than the stiff spikes of bloom of new bulbs will be the looser clusters of bulbs that have begun to "run out" in the border. Other valuable bulbs are the snowdrop, *Scilla Sibirica*, glory-of-the-snow (*Chionodoxa Luciliæ*), guinea-hen flower (*Fritillaria Meleagris*), grape hyacinth (*Muscari botryoides*), *Triteleia uniflora*, *Allium Moly*, and the wood and Spanish hyacinths (*Scilla nutans* and *campanulata*).

Taller plants that may be worked in, oftentimes best with

only a single specimen or small clump, are autumn aconite (*Aconitum autumnale*), *Yucca filamentosa*, leopard's bane (doronicum), single peonies (either herbaceous or tree), German, Japanese, and Siberian iris, as well as the yellow flag (*Iris pseudacorus*), single columbines, *Anemone Japonica*, *Hemerocallis flava*, *Sedum spectabile*, *Dielytra spectabile*, *Dielytra formosa*, Jacob's ladder (*Polemonium Richardsonii*), fraxinella, *Anthemis tinctoria*, single *Campanula persicifolia*, *Campanula rapunculoides*, *Campanula glomerata*, globe flower (trollius), snapdragon (antirrhinum), platycodon, lavender (where it is proven hardy), and musk mallow (*Malva moschata*).

Of the lilies, *Lilium Philadelphicum*, *L. elegans*, *L. speciosum*, and *L. longiflorum* are all desirable, and they thrive in partial shade, though in Japan *L. elegans* will be found standing out from the rocks in full sunshine. For peering over into the rock garden, rather than being placed in it, *L. Canadense*, *L. tigrinum*, and *L. superbum* are recommended.

A rock garden merging into woodland. A curved path is desirable, as it affords a greater number of vistas

The pick of the low shrubs are the charming *Daphne cneorum*, which flourishes better for being lifted above the ordinary

31

garden level, and *Azalea amœna*. The latter, however, should be so placed that its trying solferino does not make a bad color clash. Rhododendrons and mountain laurel fringe a rock garden well, and with one trailing juniper (*Juniperus procumbens*) will provide a great deal of the refreshing winter green.

Single roses, the species, fit in well where there is room for them. Good ones are *R. setigera, R. rubiginosa, R. Wichuraiana*, all rampant, and the low *R. blanda*. The roses would better be at or near the entrance or exit, or far enough above the rock work not to ramble over small plants.

The plants in this list cover all seasons and vary somewhat in their soil and moisture requirements. But the variation is nothing beyond the ordinary garden knowledge. Most will do better if their preferences are considered, but none is apt to perish with average care.

Alpines, as a class, would better be left to the amateur with the time, money, and disposition to specialize. Most of them take kindly to being transferred from a mile or more up in the air to sea level; the edelweiss, for one, grows here readily from seed, and the exquisitely beautiful *Gentiana acaulis* thrives in American rock gardens. But, on the whole, alpines do not do as well here as in England, where the summer climate is not so hard on them. When they flourish here, it is at the cost of a great amount of professional care.

THE WALL GARDEN

A wall garden is a perpendicular rock garden. But whereas a rock garden is of all things irregular, a wall garden has regularity. The wall need not be a straight line; it is better that one end should describe a curve, and rocks at the base may give it further irregularity. Yet it can never quite lose the air of man's handiwork. The prime object of the gardening on it is to reduce this air to a minimum.

The way to make a wall garden is to build a dry wall of rough stones—that is, a wall without mortar. Instead use soil and pack it tight in every crevice as well as behind the stones, which should be tilted back a little to carry water into the soil. This tilting may be accomplished with small stone wedges. The best kind is a five-foot retaining wall, as there is then a good body of soil behind to which the roots can reach out through the crevices. But a double-faced wall may be made, if the situation demands it, by constructing parallel lines of stones and filling in solidly with soil.

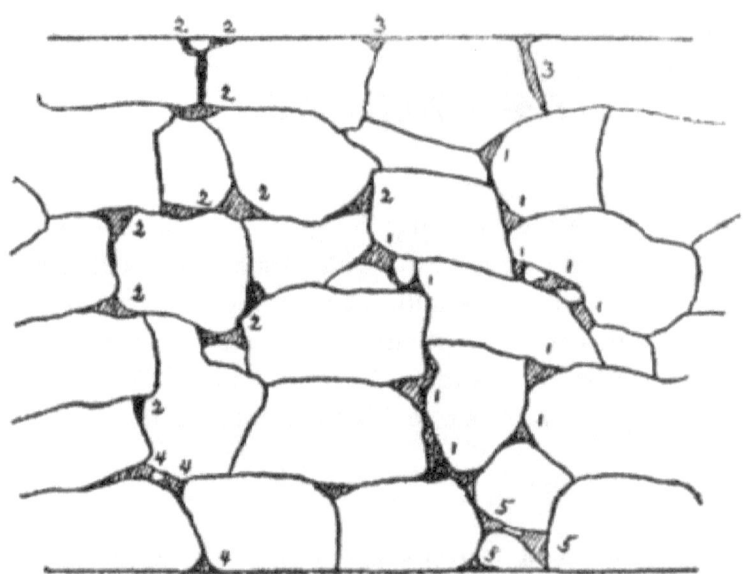

Planting plan of dry wall, the dark portions representing the chief earth-filled crevices. The plants are: 1—*Arabis albida*; 2—*Alyssum saxatile*; 3—House leek (sempervivum); 4—*Viola tricolor*; 5—*Armeria maritima*

A wall garden planted in colonies—the better way. If not too vigorous of growth, vines may be planted as shown

here at the base

Although the face of the wall in either case may be strictly perpendicular, it is better that each layer should recede a bit. Construct it after the manner of the rock garden, laying the stones so that the top will be level, or approximately so.

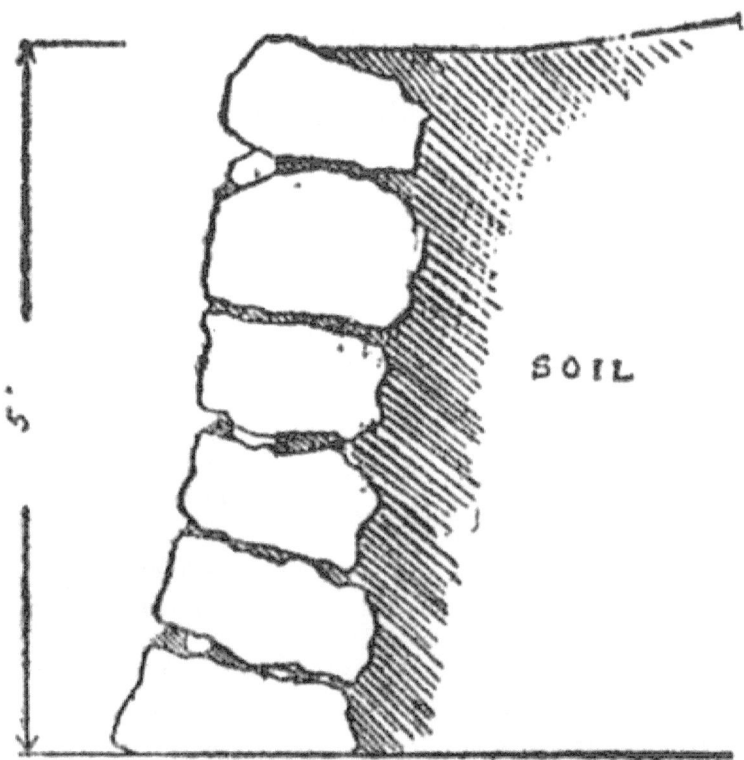

Dry wall for retaining bank. Cross-section, showing crevices, soil runs and tilting of rocks

In planting also, follow the same rules. It is better to plant as the work progresses. Either plants or seed may be used. If it is seed, press carefully into the soil in the front of the crevices. Small seed may be mixed in thin mud and this plastered on the soil. For a tiny crevice make a pill of the mixture.

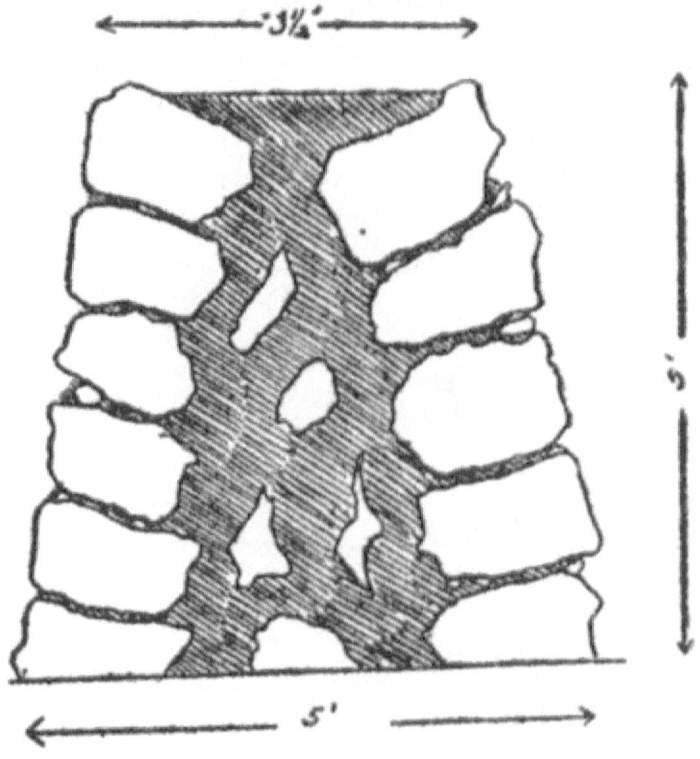

Double-faced dry wall. A few rocks are used with the soil filling and here and there one on top of it

The range of reliable plants that do not call for special care is not great so far as the crevices are concerned. All the stonecrops, the house leeks, *Arabis albida*, red valerian (*Centranthus ruber*), aubrietia, *Alyssum saxatile*, snapdragon, wallflower (*Cheiranthus Cheiri*), Kenilworth ivy, *Viola tricolor*, *Dianthus plumarius*, and *Dianthus deltoides* are all very serviceable. Behind the wall, at the top, a strip of earth should be left and there a wider variety of plants can be grown. Single Marguerite carnations and grass pinks will form a sort of cascade of foliage and bloom there if planted close to the wall or in the crevices of the top, and a similar effect, but much bolder, can be created with the perennial pea (*Lathyrus latifolius*).

If the dry wall is already made, the crevices can be plugged with soil if care and patience are used. Even a cemented wall is not hopeless; here and there the mortar can be chiseled out and an occasional small stone should be removed.

A wall garden has these advantages over a rock garden; it is more easily constructed, it is of practical use, and it is sometimes a possibility where the other is not.

WATER AND BOG GARDENS

Neither the water nor the bog garden is dependent on rocks. Either or both, however, may just as well be an adjunct of the rock garden. They solve the wet spot problem admirably, permit the culture of native water lilies, orchids, and numerous other beautiful plants, and certainly contribute their share of picturesqueness. If water is lacking, it may often be introduced at little expense.

A little grotto with trickling water makes a picturesque
break in a wall garden. If shady, plant ferns generously

In most cases it will be found that some cement construction is necessary, but not a bit of it should show. This is easily managed by building a cement shoulder on the sides of the pool or stream a little below what will be the level of the water, and then setting rough stones on that. A cement bottom for shallow water may be disguised by imbedding pebbles and small stones in the cement before it sets.

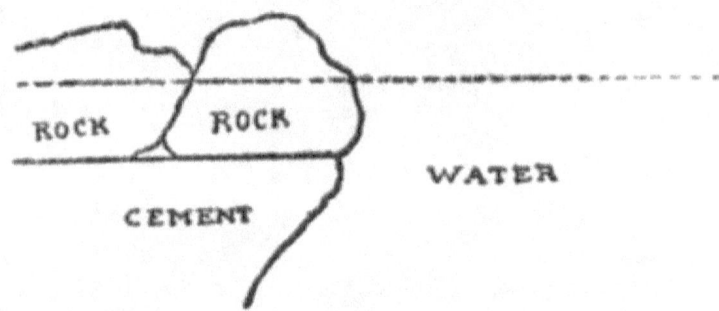

To conceal the cemented bank of a pool or stream, make a shoulder eight inches or so wide and about six inches below the water line. Then place small rocks on the shoulder

Dispose the rocks very irregularly, but they may be so few as to be mere notes. Avoid stagnant water, and if mosquitoes are feared introduce some goldfish. They like mosquito larvæ.

Water lilies and sagittaria—one plant will do if the pool is small—in the water and near it, but not in standing water, Japanese iris, yellow flag, globe flower, and *Lythrum roseum* are good selections. Forget-me-not is one of the finest plants for the banks. Use the perennial kind (*Myosotis palustris semperflorens*).

The bog garden simply reproduces bog conditions. As a rock garden adjunct it may be a small spot with the perpetually moist and moss-covered soil in which the native cypripediums and pitcher plants flourish. Eighteen or twenty inches of suitable soil, a mixture of leaf mold, peat, and loam, in which has been stirred some sand and gravel, must be provided. If an artificial bog, the bottom may be made of cement or puddled clay.

---

www.ingramcontent.com/pod-product-compliance
Lightning Source LLC
Chambersburg PA
CBHW030912260626
47169CB00008B/2813